I.G. Collins

Scinde & the Punjaub

SALZWASSER
VERLAG

I.G. Collins

Scinde & the Punjaub

Reprint of the original.

1st Edition 2023 | ISBN: 978-3-37514-386-2

Verlag (Publisher): Salzwasser Verlag GmbH, Zeilweg 44, 60439 Frankfurt, Deutschland
Vertretungsberechtigt (Authorized to represent): E. Roepke, Zeilweg 44, 60439 Frankfurt, Deutschland
Druck (Print): Books on Demand GmbH, In de Tarpen 42, 22848 Norderstedt, Deutschland

SCINDE & THE PUNJAUB,

THE GEMS OF INDIA,

IN RESPECT TO THEIR VAST AND UNPARALLELED CAPABILITIES OF
SUPPLANTING THE SLAVE STATES OF AMERICA,

IN THE

COTTON MARKETS OF THE WORLD:

OR, AN

APPEAL TO THE ENGLISH NATION

ON BEHALF OF ITS GREAT COTTON INTEREST,

THREATENED WITH INADEQUATE SUPPLIES OF THE RAW MATERIAL.

By I. G. COLLINS, Esq.,

LATE CAPTAIN, 13TH LIGHT DRAGOONS.

MANCHESTER:

A. IRELAND AND CO., PRINTERS BY STEAM POWER, PALL MALL.

1858.

TO

THE RIGHT HONORABLE LORD STANLEY, M.P.,

PRESIDENT OF THE BOARD OF CONTROL,

IN GRATEFUL ACKNOWLEDGMENT OF HIS LORDSHIP'S EMINENT PUBLIC

SERVICES FOR THE DEVELOPMENT OF THE RESOURCES OF

BRITISH INDIA

(ESPECIALLY IN REFERENCE TO THE CULTIVATION OF THE COTTON PLANT).

AND, ALSO, AS AN HUMBLE THOUGH SINCERE TRIBUTE TO HIS

LORDSHIP'S PRIVATE WORTH AND COMMANDING TALENTS,

THIS PAMPHLET IS MOST RESPECTFULLY DEDICATED

BY HIS LORDSHIP'S MOST OBEDIENT

FAITHFUL SERVANT,

THE AUTHOR.

June 14th, 1858.

SCINDE AND THE PUNJAUB,

THE GEMS OF INDIA :

AN APPEAL TO THE ENGLISH NATION

ON BEHALF OF ITS GREAT COTTON INTEREST,

THAT India can be made, by the talisman of European capital, energy, and skill, the great cotton-field
of the world, is a truth that no person, well acquainted
with the vast resources and extraordinary capabilities
of this magnificent dependency, will, for a moment,
doubt. And yet, notwithstanding the admitted fact
that Englishmen possess the means, to an unlimited
extent, of growing cotton on their own territory, at a
much less cost than in any other part of the habitable
globe, they still, with a worse than suicidal infatua-
tion, persevere in the maintenance of the most abject
and hazardous dependence upon the Slave States of
America for the chief supply of *the raw material* that
keeps in motion their ponderous mass of spindles and
looms—employs, in factories alone, four millions of
the industrial population—sustains the vast fabric of
their mercantile relations—and contributes, more than
any other known product, to the expansion of their
maritime greatness and the increase of the Govern-

ment exchequer, and the public wealth! A more anomalous condition of things than is represented by this *national* act and system of folly does not exist to jeopardise our manufacturing supremacy, or to call into question our boasted claim as a people to be considered prudent, sagacious, and enterprising.

If the consumption of raw cotton in the United Kingdom last year had been equal in all respects to that of 1856, and had not been diminished in consequence chiefly of the Sepoy mutiny and the money-panic in America, and had India not given us an increased supply, we should not, at the beginning of 1858, have had a single bale of cotton in stock. From 1816 to the present time, the stocks of cotton in ports and in the hands of consumers, have varied from eighteen weeks' supply to fifty-three weeks' supply. At the end, however, of 1855, there was only a supply for fourteen weeks; at the end of 1856, twelve weeks' supply; and in March of this very year, Mr. Henry Ashworth, in his able lecture reported in the "Journal of the Society of Arts," stated that, in that month, the stock of American cotton in Liverpool was only equal to the consumption of three weeks, and the entire stock of all kinds to a consumption of four weeks. This limited supply must, of necessity, occasion a collapse or contraction of the productive capabilities and operations of this country; and I fearlessly ask, does not this state of things, lamentable in the extreme, indicate to us the sound, rational policy of increasing at once our supplies of cotton

from all available sources, and especially from India,—
an appendage of the British crown, and the **Natal**
home of the cotton plant ?

It is terrible to contemplate the probable consequences in this country of a deficient harvest in
the Southern States of America. This is a contin-
gency that may often, or at any time, occur; and
the inevitable result of such a catastrophe would be
loss and ruin to the cotton manufacturers of Great Britain.
The slightest atmospheric epidemic on the banks of
the Mississippi may derange the entire system of our
national commerce and industry, and plunge **all**
classes into irretrievable anarchy and distress; throw
out of employment more than one-fourth of our
working population ; and cast a gloom over our commercial destinies which years of unusual prosperity
could alone dissipate. But, had we a supply from
other sources, a bad harvest in one quarter might be
compensated by a good one in another; whereas,
by depending upon a *single* source, and to make
matters worse, a *foreign* source, we are liable to
suffer from a thousand casualties. A deficient crop,
a slave insurrection, or a diplomatic blunder, occur-
ing thousands of miles from our shores, and among
a rival nation, may suddenly, but fatally, put an end
to our manufacturing supremacy, and lay the proud
fabric of our commercial greatness level with the dust,
never to rise again !

Besides which, if (as is alleged by the most competent authorities) the cotton-growing districts of the

United States has nearly, if not altogether, "reached the maximum, the highest attainable limit, of their productive power, and that they cannot calculate upon growing any considerable quantity beyond the amount of their present average crops," either a new source of supply must be opened equal to the requirements of the cotton manufacturers of Great Britain, or the British cotton industry has also reached its culminating point; or must henceforth recede, for to remain stationary is, according to all the parallelisms of history, impossible, for nations, trades, or arts.

Were America to do us a grievous wrong in the face of all Europe and of the world, we dare not go to war with her, for on her alone are we dependent for the fibre, which, startling as the fact may appear, maintains our mighty fleets on every sea, and gives employment to industry, activity to commerce, and revenue to the State. But, I ask, is this deplorable state of things a *necessity* to which England *must* submit? Has she no means of emancipating herself from this abject dependence, worse than vassalage? Cannot she grow cotton in her own dominions amply sufficient to meet all her demands? Has she not in British India, on the banks of the Indus, a congenial soil, cheap labour, and abundant means of river and railway transit at command and constantly extending, and every known requisite—except English capital and skill—for the profitable cultivation of the cotton plant? Most decidedly she has—and the "East India Cotton Company" is the agency proposed by me to work out her redemption, and to enable her no longer to fear the frown of an American President, who is said to "hold a power over us, a rod *in terrorem,*—more to be dreaded, and which would prove far more effective in compelling a premature and involuntary peace, than all the fleets and armies that can be brought against us." "America," continues the author of the "Cotton Crisis," "could stop the supply of cotton, and thereby ruin our commerce, shut up our factories, and bring a pressure to bear upon the Government which would compel them to *sue for peace, even though the national honour should demand the prosecution of the war.*"

But there is another consideration having immediate reference to our state of dependence on America, which, in the bosoms of the humane, benevolent, and patriotic, must tend to excite emotions too painful and humiliating for words fully to express. England's demand for slave-grown cotton is the secret of American slavery, and the great cause of that eager pertinacity with which the descendants of Washington, Jefferson, and Franklin cling to the perpetuation of a system of oppression, spoliation, and wrong, openly acknowledged to be at variance with all the principles of humanity, civilisation, and justice. "All American statesmen," says a writer in the *Times* newspaper, "and political economists throughout the world understand that nothing has rooted negro slavery in America so deeply, or promised it so long an existence as the profit arising from the culture of cotton, and the inability of England, France, and Germany to obtain supplies from any other quarter for their great manufactories."

The following curt, though pertinent and truthful, remarks on this subject are from the pen of a former overseer, or slave driver, on an American plantation, but who was so shocked with the system of cruelty perpetrated daily under his immediate observation that he indignantly threw up his employment, and is now actively at work superintending the culture of cotton by free labour on the soil of Africa, under the direct auspices of that best, because the most practical, of philanthropists—Thomas Clegg, Esq., of Manchester :—

"The foul monster of slavery is maintained through *Great Britain's purchasing American cotton.* Slavery allows professing Christians to sell their own children; slavery permits ministers of the gospel to separate husbands and wives; a loving mother from the child of her bosom. Slavery shuts out the light of heaven from the human soul; it whips religion away from the cotton farm; it prostitutes mothers, daughters, and sisters; it leads the slaveholder to say to his victim, 'Have I not bought your flesh, every pound of it? Have I not paid down my money for it? Have I not a right to whip, and chain, and drop hot sealing wax upon it, if I please? Have I not bought every drop of blood in your body, and paid for it, and don't owe a dollar on it? What sneak of an abolitionist dares to inquire into the internal management of my slavedom ? Am I not living in the land of freedom—in the freest country in the world, where a man can raise and sell his own children according to law? Am I not on my own plantation, walled in by gags and gag-laws? Have I not my own grave-yard, my stocks, irons, &c.? Who dare even question my constitutional right to torture my own nigger, made to grow cotton for the master race, and for nothing else? Even England would perish if you black rascals did not make her a supply of cotton!' 'Dat am fact, massa,' would be the probable reply. I say again, that you, as a nation, could soon strike the chains for ever from the slave, and you may do so without going to war, or getting into any other difficulty with any power upon earth. Now is the time for all Christian and philanthropic men to awake to their duty. The effort would cost you less money than your ships of war upon the coast of Africa. Start this ball, and keep it in motion until a permanent free-labour cotton supply has been established. Build your hopes, for the future, on a solid basis, that no chartered monopolist can control or undermine. Then will the slave-driver be unable to shout defiance, or to hurrah for slave-labour cotton, crying 'Cotton is King! Cotton rules Britannia! If we were to keep back one year's crop, we should have England upon her knees.' Yes! proud and haughty John Bull upon his knees to the American slave-driver."

Well may the writer indignantly ask,—"Christian-professing England, where is thy brother? Wilt thou be guiltless of his blood on that terrible day? Even now a cotton famine may suddenly stare thee in the face. Some unlooked for occurrence may deprive thee of the accustomed supply. Thy children will then cry for bread. Revolution and disorganisation will ensue. Thy commerce will be arrested. Thy proud wooden walls will be swept from the seas. ' How is the mighty fallen,' will be the derisive cry; and Great Britain will become the laugh and scorn of her rivals."

The preceding remarks fully bear me out in the opinion I have long entertained, that the crime of American slavery lies quite as much at the doors of the English cotton spinners as of the cotton planters of the "South." England's continued prosperity depends on her cotton manufactures; and these, in their turn, owing to the culpable apathy of the English manufacturers, depend on a rival nation for an adequate supply of the raw material—the product of slavery in its worst form, and reared at the cost of all that humanity holds dear and sacred. The Rev. R. Earnest, in his "Journey through the United States," emphatically and truly says that "every new factory built in Lancashire creates a demand for slaves on the banks of the Mississippi." I ask, is this state of things to continue? Disciples of Penn and Fox! you who have ever been honourably distinguished for your uncompromising crusade against all wrong, bloodshed, and oppression, will you not rally to the *cause of freedom*, consecrated by the labours of a Wilberforce, a Clarkson, and Fowell Buxton, and by throwing in your influence and capital to help on, to a successful issue, the " East India Cotton Company," prove to the satisfaction of America and the world that cotton *can* be grown on the banks of the Indus, *by free labour*, at a less cost, and with a greater profit, than it can be in New Orleans, or Mobile, or Arkansas, although out of the very groans and life-blood of the oppressed and goaded slave? Christians! 1 invite your co-operation to regenerate, civilise, and Christianise India; to put down slavery in its most disgusting and selfish forms; and to ensure the continued prosperity of England by opening up to her new sources of supply of that material without which her commerce, industry, and all her social and religious institutions, must necessarily collapse, and terminate in one wholesale catastrophe of ruin, bankruptcy, and national disorganisation. Cotton spinners of Lancashire! to you I appeal for support on economical considerations alone, because your boasted prosperity is daily at the mercy of a rival nation, and may be scattered to the winds by the first atmospheric epidemic that may sweep, with mysterious pungency, the cotton plantations of the "far South." Grow cotton by free labour in India—your own territory—and COMBINE your capital, intelligence, and enterprise for that noble, as well as profitable, object, and that moment you " strike a blow against American slavery that shall be felt in a day from the

Potomac to the Rio Grande." "For upwards of twenty years," exclaims the writer previously quoted, " all the moral power of the abolitionists of the world has been levelled against this institution ; but, up to the present hour, I think it would be difficult to show that 1,000 slaves have, through their influence, been emancipated in the United States, while the number has increased more than 1,000,000." One £10 note, invested in the " East India Cotton Company," will do more to put an end to the slave trade, whose horrors have been so ably portrayed by the celebrated Mrs. Stowe, than double that sum contributed as a mere donation to an " Anti-Slavery Society," or deposited in the hands of the sentimental " philanthropists of Stafford-House." For " no doubt whatever can be entertained that the South will relax its grasp upon the slave the very moment the hold ceases to be profitable : but so long as cotton is selling for 500 dollars a bale, and negroes are worth from 1,000 to 1,500 dollars, all the preaching, and all the entreaty, and all the schemes for the emancipation of the American slave, will be as fruitless as ' the whistling wind.' " I repeat, that as soon as cotton is grown in sufficient quantities, and at a fair profit, on the banks of the Indus, either in the Scinde or Punjaub territory, or in both, by free adult labour, that moment the " slavery of the South" will cease to be either a necessity or an expediency, *and America will be free !* The arrival in India of the agents of the " East India Cotton Company" will not merely contribute to the permanence and beneficence of our sovereign's rule in that magnificent empire, but they will inaugurate a brighter era in the freedom of the human race, either on the shores of the Mississippi, or on the coasts of Africa from whence poor wretches are still liable to be stolen to gratify the cupidity of their "white brethren" in distant lands, than has ever yet been accomplished by the mere efforts of abolition-societies and eleemosynary charities, or can by any other means whatever be accomplished. Governor Adams, in his message to the South Carolina Legislature, of the 24th of November last, recognised a fact of this kind in the following emphatic words :—" *Destroy the value of slave-labour, and emancipation follows inevitably.*" And again, where he says—" The consumption of cotton has steadily increased, and will in a few years exceed the supply. The prices must go up in the absence of all disturbing causes ; as long as this continues to be the case, we must prosper, but the certain effect of high prices will be to stimulate the growth of cotton in foreign countries, and, in time, to destroy the monopoly which we have so long enjoyed. The possession of this monopoly is the chief element of Southern prosperity, and the dependence of the manufacturing interest upon us for a supply of this article, will continue to prove to be one of our strongest safeguards."

Notwithstanding this complacent prediction on the part of Governor Adams, the slave-system he advocates is secretly but surely undermining the agricultural prosperity of the cotton-growing States. The Superintendent of the Banking Department of New York, in his Annual Report to the State Legislature, mentions the singular though startling fact, that whilst the manufacturing towns or localities had greatly increased in population and wealth, the agricultural districts had either in these respects remained stationary or declined. This could not have happened under any other system than that of slavery, or, as it is called, "compulsory servitude." The difficulty in providing a sufficiency of negro labour renders it extremely improbable that any much greater area of cotton land can be cultivated in the "South." For already have complaints been made of an inadequacy in the slave population to keep pace with the requirements of the cotton planters, and, through them, of the cotton spinners of Great Britain and Continental Europe. Hence it is that the value of slaves has risen to such an extravagant height in the market, as almost to appear fabulous to a European. An immense capital is required by the planter to obtain a sufficient number of labourers on the soil; whereas, the Indian cultivator can hire adult labour to any extent at 3d. or 4d. per diem. The same labour will cost the American slave-owner two shillings per diem.

I may remark, by way of conclusion, on this subject, that I do not urge or advocate the *immediate* liberation of the slave in the Southern States of America. Such a step requires to be gradual in its operations, because, were it suddenly adopted, the slaves themselves would suffer to an extent beyond

our power fully to comprehend. The first movement
made to prepare the negro population for a general
emancipation, should consist in a complete revi-
sion of the present inhuman code of laws, which
forbids them from being admitted evidence in what
are now styled, by way of mockery, *Courts of
Justice!* Inspectors or Commissioners should be
appointed by the Executive Government, to visit
periodically, or at such times as they may think
proper, the whole of the slave-owning States, for
the purpose of ascertaining if any undue severity has
been practised by planter or overseer, and, for every
outrage on decency and humanity, to bring the
offender before a violated tribunal. This system, if
faithfully carried out, would have the effect of pre-
paring the down-trodden race for the *certain consequences* of their liberation, and their assumption of the
rights and responsibilities of citizenship. It would
accustom them to look up to the State for protection,
and they would soon cease to regard their employers
as oppressors and torturers; nay, to the contrary,
feelings of self-respect, and gratitude towards them,
would gradually spring up in their minds. While
thus being prepared for freedom, a certain number
of the most intelligent among them might be placed
in Government or other offices, for the purpose of
being trained to superintend and direct their brethren
when emancipated. Eventually, a portion of them
might be freed in each State, with a guarantee of
one year's food; and these might also be furnished

with requisite implements for the cultivation of, and settlement on, certain grants of land, under the care of white protectors, who, in process of time, would be aided in the discharge of their duties by those blacks previously emancipated, and selected for the purpose. In this way they would, doubtless, gradually settle down into a respectable and well-conducted colony. Missionaries and ministers of religion would gladly volunteer their services, in order to prepare the negro for this happy change in his condition.

By these means, the time would soon arrive (especially if their number should dwindle down to half the white population in the South) when they might be *emancipated without danger*. To a superficial thinker, it might appear folly to expect that a period so lengthened of cruelty the most aggravated, oppression the most wanton, and outrage the most malignant ever practised, could be obliterated from the minds of these " hereditary victims ;" but it must be remembered that the negro character has little stability, is essentially vain and frivolous, and yet none the less grateful and affectionate. Once that justice be done to this ill-treated people— security from wrong, and equal rights in Courts of Law, with a fair remuneration for their labour, and, mere children of impulse as they confessedly are, their social and moral improvement would become gradually and distinctly perceptible to the most obtuse observer. Their *emancipation*, under such a preparatory training, could be effected without either danger to the State or to themselves as recipients. And what period for such an event could be more auspicious and congenial than the celebration of that day when " peace on earth and good-will to man" was first proclaimed to the world,—time-honoured Christmas ? Having been gradually prepared for the boon of liberty, they would accept moderate wages for their labour, and, it is my firm impression, would ultimately settle down into more valuable workmen, at a less cost considerably *than now*. To hasten "a consummation so devoutly to be wished," let me call upon every Christian in the empire, and upon all friends of humanity, to unite with me in the righteous crusade I have proposed to wage, by weapons the most effective and economical, for the suppression of the American Slave trade. This object can only be attained by a plentiful supply of *free-labour cotton*, and by convincing the planter of the South that slave labour is more costly and less valuable than that of *free-men*, and that, by means of the former, he stands a fair chance of losing his present position in respect to the European cotton markets. Every pulpit in this Christian land should ring with anathemas of that traffic in human beings which is the open disgrace of the Americans; and is as revolting in detail, as it is unjust in principle.

According to the " New York Shipping and Commercial List," there was a decrease in the export to foreign ports in the year dating from September 1st,

B

1856, to August 1st, 1857, compared with the total export of the year preceding, of 701,949 bales, distributed thus :—

Decrease to	Great Britain............	492,516 bales.
,,	France	67,280 ,,
,,	North of Europe	58,207 ,,
,,	other foreign ports....	83,946 ,,

Total decrease of export .... 701,949 ,,

The total amount of cotton exported in the former period being 2,252,657 bales, and in the year preceding 2,954,606 bales.

The comparative statement of growth shows also a decrease :—

Crop of 1855-6...............	3,527,845 bales.
,, 1856-7...............	2,939,519 ,,

Decrease of growth .... 588,326 ,,

Notwithstanding this decrease in the growth, facts show an increase in the American consumption of 13,623 bales. In 1855-6, the surplus over the export kept for the home manufactures was 573,239 bales, and in 1856-7, 686,862 bales,—a not very satisfactory state of things to be contemplated by either the English or European competitor! In short, taking the above authority as our guide, the whole consumption of the United States, in the year dating to September 1st, 1857, was 840,000 bales, against 788,000 bales the year before. So that while Europe has had to put up with a deficiency, owing to a decrease in the crop,

the American manufacturers obtained a veritable
increase of the raw material by being the *purchasers
on the spot*, and thus possessing an advantage to the
detriment of the English consumers, as competitors
with them in the markets of the world.

And what is the result of all this ? Why, a double
injury to the industrial and mercantile interests of
Great Britain! Not merely do we find in the Americans,
successful competitors in markets once our exclusive
possession in the sale of cotton manufactured goods,
but we have to pay them a few millions sterling
every year in excess of the legitimate working-value
of the raw material we are compelled to obtain from
them, having ourselves utterly neglected the cultivation
of cotton, *on an extensive and remunerative basis*, in our
vast Indian dominions. No wonder that the rise in
the price of American cotton, in 1857, affected inju-
riously the whole of our community. In the middle
of last year it is well known that the average price of
the kind of cotton most in demand was 8d. per ℔,
whereas the same cotton had, not very long before,
been purchased at half that price. And let the
reader bear in mind that every increase of one penny
per ℔ in the price of this fibre causes a *bona fide* loss
to this country of £4,250,000, or not much less than
the whole amount of the income tax of Sir Robert Peel
when it was first levied. Hence Lord Stanley calcu-
lated, and broadly asserted in the Manchester Town
Hall last year, that the increase in price to which the
cotton spinners had been then obliged to submit

amounted to no less a sum than *seventeen millions sterling per annum ;* and yet these very men have not had the wisdom and enterprise to devote a portion of their surplus capital to the cultivation of cotton in India, where there are almost innumerable collectorates capable of producing more cotton, at a cheaper rate, even from New Orleans seed, than the whole of the United States.* Surely their deplorable apathy will now come to an end, when, with a very moderate investment each, they can carry into execution the grandest organisation ever yet formed (or even proposed) for the purpose of freeing themselves from their present suicidal dependence on the slave-owners of America, and of supplying their own wants from the banks of the Indus, rather than from the shores of the Mississippi. By joining the "East India Cotton Company" they can, in an incredibly short period, assume that supremacy in the cotton trade to which England by her position is so well entitled, as well as remove from their own trade—the staple textile industry of Great Britain —a tax virtually of sixteen or seventeen millions per annum, and give enlarged scope and *stamina* to the progressive expansion of English commerce and of English manufactures.

If the reader of this pamphlet be disposed to apprehend no material danger to our commercial or political destinies, arising from the maintenance of our present humiliating dependence on America, and by neglecting to combine for the extended growth of

* See Appendix.

cotton in British dominions, let him ponder well over the following extract from Mr. Mackay's " Western India" :—

"As regards the supply of cotton, we are as much at the mercy of America as if we were starving, and to her alone we looked for food. She need not withhold her wheat; she could starve us by withholding her cotton. True, it is as much her interest as ours to act differently; and, so long as it continues so, no difficulty will be experienced. But a combination of circumstances may be supposed, in which America, at little cost to herself, might strike us an irrecoverable blow. A crisis may arrive when, by momentarily crippling our industry, she may push in and deprive us of the markets of the world: and who, should the opportunity arise, will guarantee her forbearance? Fill England with provisions, let her harbours be choked, and her granaries bursting with their stores, what a spectacle would she present in a stoppage of one year's supply of cotton! It would do more to prostrate her in the dust than all the armaments which America and Europe combined could hurl against her. What a tremendous power is this in the hands of a rival! The day may come when, even should inclination be dead, self-interest may drive her to the policy of shutting up our English factories, and crushing our English trade. She has, as it were, at her command, the great dam from which all our motive power is derived, and has only to close the sluices when she wishes our machinery to stop. It is the consciousness of this absolute dependence that induces many to look anxiously elsewhere for the supply of that for which we are now wholly beholden to a rival. *The cultivation of cotton in India is no chimera. The time may come when we may find it our safety.*"

The growth of American manufactures threatens England, not merely with a diminution in her exports of textile fabrics to that country, but also with a formidable competition for the cotton produced by slave labour there; and, also, in the best markets of the world wherein British goods have, for more than a century, held undisputed possession. It is in the power of English capitalists, whilst at the same time gaining large, nay, unparalleled, profits, to make India do more for us than America has done, or is capable of doing. For it is in their power to grow cotton on the banks of the Indus more than sufficient to meet all the manufacturing requirements at home, and to convert the teeming millions of our Eastern empire into the largest and best customers for the fabrics spun and woven from Indian cotton by the skilful operatives of Manchester, Glasgow, and other seats of our staple industry. Nay, further, it is in their power, whilst ameliorating, directly or remotely, the physical and social condition of more than 150 millions of our fellow-subjects, to free the cotton trade of this kingdom from its present hazardous dependence on a foreign state for a supply of the fibrous substance necessary to its very sustentation.

not to speak of its future developments and unlimited powers of expansion, aided, doubtless, by new contrivances of mechanical art, and the equally remarkable discoveries of practical science. When we consider that India contains 200 millions of inhabitants, and that they each consume on an average 12lb of cotton (the men wearing pretty nearly the same habiliments as the women), it will be evident to the most superficial thinker what an immense opening this magnificent country will present to the future operations of the English manufacturers, when once converted into their *great cotton-field*, and its vast resources developed under a mild and paternal Government!

The value of British goods exported at the present time to India is ridiculously small when compared with the quantities exported to the mixed population of South America, or even to our West India Islands. Nay, our exports to India are of less value by six millions sterling per annum than to our Australian colonies. Hence, says Mr. Chapman, "If India consumed our goods at the same rate as South America, we should export to India as much as we now export to *all the rest of the world.*" What a field is there here for future English enterprise! To what a colossal magnitude our commerce with India may yet grow! Even if we are threatened in the continental and other markets with a competition most damaging to our prospects as a manufacturing nation, a more than a counterpoise exists in British India, with her *hundreds of millions,* all capable of being clothed with fabrics made in England from the very cotton grown by themselves, and originally purchased from them, it may be, by the agents of the "East India Cotton Company."

Sir Thos. Munroe (one of the most able governors that Madras ever had) informs us that the inability of the people to consume English manufactures arises, not from want of inclination, but from sheer poverty. "It is a mistaken notion," he says, "that Indians are too simple in their manners to have any passion for foreign manufactures. In dress, and every kind of dissipation but drinking, they are at least our equals"—that is, had they the ability to purchase or obtain our fabrics in exchange for the raw cotton they produce ; and, by obtaining their raw cotton, you provide them with the means of gratifying their passion to purchase British manufactures.

We have it on a most competent authority in India, that " of the value of the whole exports of the manufactures of England, little more than one-tenth portion comes to British India, while the exports of India, exclusive of China and the Eastern Islands, are £12,000,000 of productions."*

If, indeed, it be true (as is alleged by our political economists) that the primary object of our Government and our merchants should be to find new customers for English manufactures, or, what amounts to the same thing, to increase the demand in those

* See " Cotton Crisis," page 17.

quarters where British commerce has already evolved
the elements of civilisation, then India, of a truth,
offers the most attractive field for enterprise, and in
this respect outrivals all our other dependencies and
possessions put together, in the number of its inhabitants, and the immense facilities of commercial intercourse and traffic it holds out to the acceptance and
vast benefit of British manufacturers and capitalists;
and at no period since Lord Clive first planted the
British flag on the walls of Calcutta, and expanded a
factory into an empire, has the truth been so generally
conceded as now, that the interests of England and
India are inseparable; and that they are destined to
act and re-act upon each other with omnipotent
energy for good or ill, just according to the direction
given by the Indian Government to an enlightened
or a destructive policy, and by English capitalists
generally to an organised system of profitable enterprise, or a continued ruinous neglect of all practical
and sound means of industrial development.

A writer in the "Westminster Review" has very
pertinently and philosophically remarked that,
"whatever obstructs the extension of our Indian
commerce has a tenfold importance, from its equally
obstructing the real improvement of the Indian
people."

Emigration to India, under the direct auspices of
a paternal government, would, I feel convinced, be
attended with the best possible results. Hence, in
another part of this pamphlet, the reader will learn that

some months ago I had the honour to address the East
India Company* on this subject, and then suggested
that encouragement should be given to those of the
humbler classes in England who are disposed to
settle in India. The military emigration system
practised by the Government at the Cape of Good
Hope in respect to the German Legion, has answered
exceedingly. A similar plan might be properly
carried into effect in the more temperate parts or
hilly districts of British India. I firmly believe that
many pensioners and discharged soldiers of excellent
character, not exceeding a certain age, who could
furnish certificates of good conduct from their late
regiments, or from the clergymen and magistrates of
their present places of residence, would be tempted to
emigrate in large numbers if small grants of land (held
by military tenure, not transferable until the expiration
of a certain fixed period of occupancy) were guaran-
teed to them, on their engaging to do garrison duty
when called upon by the Government. By this simple
means a large European force, at comparatively a
small cost, would be permanently located on the banks
of the Indus or elsewhere, and if any commotion took
place in a remote province, the regular troops could
be sent to the scene of action, because the emigrant-
settlers would be liable to be called in to do garrison
duty. These Europeans would also set an example
to the natives of skill and industry, and form ties of
friendship and amity with them, thus contributing,

* See Appendix.

perhaps more effectually than may at first glance be thought possible, † the peace and tranquillity, as well as to the industrial and social improvement, of the Indian people. Had this plan been adopted many years ago, what an immensity of blood and treasure might have been spared! Perhaps, the fearful mutiny that has overrun the plains of Bengal would never have happened had there been a large white population living in daily intercourse with the natives, and teaching them some of our more enlightened usages and Christian virtues. An improved system of juris-prudence would, at any rate, in this case have been established, and better institutions of a public kind would have gradually sprung up in those provinces *peopled by Europeans.*

It is true that, should pensioners and discharged soldiers be encouraged to emigrate to India, the Government would have to find funds, in the first instance, to enable them to cultivate the land. Such advances, however, could be secured by first mortgage on the crops, as the ryots are accustomed to do when the soil or its produce is free from Government claims. These settlers would, in all probability, become in time extensive cotton-planters, and employ large portions of the native population in various industrial processes, as, of course, they could not be expected to labour with their own hands, owing to the intense heat of the sun, but mainly superintend and direct agricultural and other operations.

W. P. Andrew, Esq., the father of the Indian

Railways, and well known for his untiring efforts to develope the vast resources of this great peninsula, states that " the plains of India are unfit for European settlers, further than as masters of labourers : but in the capacity of coffee, indigo, *and, above all, cotton-planters*, zemindars, manufacturers, clerks, master artificers, contractors, tradesmen, there is room for an enormous increase of numbers, *and every encouragement ought to be given to their settling in the country.* The Himalayan and inter-Himalayan regions are wonderfully adapted for the European constitution. Europeans can, if they choose, work in the open air, in proof of which it is stated that the strongest built house at one of the hill stations was constructed entirely by European soldiers, without any native aid whatever."

India stands alone in this, that she has fewer emigrants from the dominant country settled within her borders than any other dependency or colony in the world. Compare her in this respect with Algeria ! At the latter, its most enterprising residents are Frenchmen, proud that they are still living under the protection of the Imperial *regime*, and determined to make the colony of their choice a great *cotton-field for France.* The primary fault of the East India Company has been that they have given no encouragement (until, perhaps, very lately) to English enterprise, with a view to develope the extraordinary resources of certainly the finest and most tempting territory under the sun. It is to this cause that is to be attributed the non-colonisation of India up to the present time. Had proper inducements been held out, and had wise laws been established, Anglo-Saxon skill, industry, and energy would long ere this have converted the Scinde and Punjaub into one great cotton-plantation, capable of supplying Great Britain with all the cotton her spindles and looms can consume.

Within the last few years, three millions of our people have emigrated ; but out of this vast number scarcely any have gone to India, although confessedly the largest and richest country to which they could possibly embark and apply the talisman of their capital and labour.

In 1853, there were only 317 British subjects, unconnected with the East India Company, engaged in agricultural or commercial pursuits in the three great Presidencies of India, which were distributed as follows :—

Bengal...................................... 273
Madras 37
Bombay 7

This state of things fully bears out Henry Ashworth, Esq., in his statement that, " So far as can be gathered of the policy of India, the effect has not been to encourage European enterprise and capital employed in the cultivation of the soil." Were English money and skill, however, directed to the growth and purchase of cotton in India, not merely would great profits be made, but both India and Great Britain would be largely benefited. A

better era already promises to dawn on the agricultural, commercial, and political destinies of our great
Eastern empire. Mr. Ewart's Colonisation Committee,
and the proposed transfer of India from the East India
Company to the Crown, are, in the estimation of many,
cheering indications of a willingness, on the part of
those who have now to do with the Indian Government, to encourage for the future the investment of
English wealth and enterprise in the cultivation of the
soil of India,—and, for this purpose, to make grants
of land *in perpetuity* in those cases where there is a
sufficiency of capital to ensure success. But even in
the absence of such grants, it is contended by a late
Government collector in the South Mahratta country,
that the cultivator of cotton in India is placed under
no disadvantage, as compared with his rival in
America, on account of the additional burden im-
posed upon the land in the shape of rent, or rather,
of taxation. "The only payment," says he, "to
which cotton-lands are liable is the ryotwar, a small
annual assessment, varying from 1 to 1½ rupee per
acre. Assuming, then, that the American planter
gets his land for nothing (a very questionable admis-
sion), and that the Indian ryot has to pay a tax or
feu of from 2s. to 3s. per acre, still the higher price
of labour in the United States, together with the
additional cost of clearing and cultivating the land,
and transporting the produce, perhaps, some hundreds of miles to the nearest seaport, will more than
compensate for this trifling advantage." The average

cost of growing cotton in India is 3s. per acre for labour, and 3s. for land, making a total only of 6s. per acre. Cotton cannot be produced in America, with all the most favourable appliances, for eight times that sum per acre, or much under £3.

How is it then, perhaps the reader will here naturally inquire, that so little cotton is grown in India as compared with America, when it can be produced (as you say) at such a trifling cost, and in unlimited quantities? The secret is to be found in the control —in other words, the social despotism—exercised by the exorbitant money-lenders, who grasp or monopolise the fruit of the ryots' industry. " This despotism," remarks a missionary lately returned from that country, " has produced, and still continues to produce, such a feeling of apathy and depression, that, in despair of ever freeing themselves from this galling chain, the cultivators of the soil direct the little energy that is left them to the mere wants of life, *a plate of rice and a cotton rag*." It is absurd to expect an adequate supply of cotton for our wants, from India, so long as the native money-lender is permitted to hover over his victims like a vampire, ready to suck out every drop of blood, except what will just keep body and soul together. The poor ryot, according to the system that prevails in the cotton districts, is even under a bond to sell the produce of his fields to his oppressor, at whatever price the latter may choose to fix, and, if he dares to refuse, the prison doors are ready to shut on him, and his family *must starve*.

" The East India Cotton Company" is intended, to a great extent, to put down this infamous and injurious system, and, for this purpose, will instruct its agents to pay off (in certain approved cases) the claims of these usurers, and to supply the cultivators of cotton, who are known to be the most skilful and industrious of their class, with money, at a reasonable rate of interest, in the shape of an advance of two-thirds on the value of the cotton crop *when maturing*. And in respect to the native merchants or dealers in cotton, to exchange British manufactures with them for all the good and clean cotton they can collect. This mode of operation, pursued on a broad and remunerative basis, would, with all the facilities the Imperial Government would, doubtless, render to such a powerful association of capitalists, give an impetus to the cultivation of cotton, both indigenous and *from American seed*, throughout nearly the whole of India, that would soon convert its ample and prolific soil into the *great cotton-field of the world*.

A recent writer says :—

" It is universally acknowledged, by all the Indian authorities, as well as by men capable of giving an opinion, the result of personal experience, that British skill and capital are required, when any great improvement is to be effected in the quantity and quality of articles produced in India by the native population ; nor is this opinion confined to theory, we have its practical results in Bengal, where indigo, silk, sugar, and other articles of export, have all benefited in the most unmistakeable manner by such European connection.

" This would be equally the case with cotton, which is at present generally raised by advances made by native bankers to the ryots, who act on the principle of getting the greatest possible amount of profit out of the smallest possible amount of advance. By this system, the impoverished ryot is just able to keep alive the production of cotton in its lowest grade : he is unprovided with proper implements, he cannot procure a variety of seed, he dare not try experiments with even a certainty of his making his crop more valuable, he has no stimulus to induce him to watch its cultivation, keep his ground clean by weeding and the like ; his crop is always pledged and usually sold before it is picked, and no advantage is offered to him for improving its quality ; accustomed merely to eke out an addition to his scanty means of subsistence from cotton cultivation, the idea of realising a profit on his labour in excess does not exist.

"The value of his crop received by the ryot does not exceed 1d. per ℔. The middleman who deals direct with the ryot increases his profits and deteriorates the cotton by fraudulent additions, which gives the dirty character to Indian cotton in the English market : on this point Mr. Vaupell, for many years connected with the cotton trade, states to the Agricultural Society of Bombay, the cotton as it comes from the gin is beautifully clean, and if forthwith taken to the screws and packed in bales, would be all that could be desired, but it is generally put into barkees or dokias (large or gunney cloth bags), and is adulterated with seed, cotton in seed, fine sand, or finely-powdered salt, scattered over it at intervals. Another mode of adulteration is by having the entire area of the yard or court daily fresh cow-dunged about sunset, and the cotton, as it comes from the churkas, spread thereon before the ground is half dry ; the dews of night are then allowed to fall on it, and early next morning, before the sun is up, it is packed in bales, this process, besides tinging and soiling the cotton with the wet cow-dung and earth, adds considerably to the weight of the article, while it materially injures it both in fibre and cleanliness ; he adds, it is not the cultivator, but the agents employed between the grower and exporter, who find their interest in adulterating the cotton.

"The result of this wretched system, now in use, may be summed up as follows :—

"1. Capital is scantily supplied, at an enormous rate of interest.

"2. A large profit is taken by the middleman, who deals direct with the ryot : another large profit is taken by the native banker, who makes advances ; and another large profit is taken by the native merchant, who sells it to the exporter.

C

"3. Both the quantity and quality produced is greatly inferior to what it might be.

"4. The cultivation of the plant, the gathering of the cotton, its cleaning and packing, careless in the extreme ; the cultivator having no interest in the out-turn of his crop.

"5. There is no certain annual demand for cotton fit for the English manufacturer ; the general production is to suit the native manufacturer.

" It is, however, a hopeful feature in this cultivation, that the natives themselves are perfectly aware of the low quality of their cotton, and only demand a more liberal system of advances, and the certainty of having a market on the spot for the finest quality of their produce, to ensure such an improvement in the article as will render it fit for general consumption by the English manufacturer. Here, again, we are not left to theory or doubt, for the experiments made in cotton cultivation, by order of the East India Government, show, that double the quantity of a much more valuable cotton can be grown in India on the acre ; proving that the natives are correct in their anticipations of what they could do under more favourable circumstances. Dr. Royle gives the result of various sales of the experimental cotton, which are satisfactory as proving that a better system of cultivation makes Indian cotton considerably more valuable in the English market."

In addition to the ryotwar system, and its intimate connection with the money-lenders who grasp and despotically appropriate to themselves the produce of the soil, there is another deterrent cause to a greatly-extended cultivation of the cotton plant in India, and that is, the acknowledged want of, or great ignorance respecting, what is called in this country— irrigation.

It is an admitted fact that where the means of irrigation are ample, and the necessary information is possessed by the cultivator as to its efficient application to purposes of culture, the quantity of cotton grown is increased at least eight-fold, and its quality is likewise improved at the rate of 150 per cent. "In Syria," says Dr. Ure, "the cotton plant is treated in the same manner as the vine, and it yields every year a good crop, by means of ploughing and irrigation." And we are informed by Lieutenant-Colonel Grant* that, "in Abyssinia, the cotton plant varies according to the locality and supply of water, from three feet in height to upwards of seven feet. In Egypt, it is entirely grown by irrigation; and in some experiments tried by Captain Lawford, of the Madras Engineers, the produce was matured, under watering, in half the time, and was 500 per cent greater."

The province of Scinde (proposed by me as the most eligible site in India for a successful experiment in the cultivation of the cotton plant, on the part of the "East India Cotton Company") possesses ample and almost unparalleled facilities for irrigation,—the whole of the province, from Shikarpore or Sukker, on the Indus, to the sea, a distance of between 300 and 400 miles, being directly intersected by the River Indus. The right and left banks of this noble river are both admirably adapted for the growth of cotton, and possess the three great requisites,—viz., a rich soil, a hot sun, and plenty of water. Hence, Lieutenant-Colonel Grant, an eminent Indian authority and from whom I have just quoted, most ably demonstrates—as a necessary inference from his own premises—that in my selection of this province for

* See his pamphlet on "Indian Irrigation," page 8.

the first active operations of the "Company" (which I have the honour to endeavour to establish in this country), I have exercised—in this respect at least— a correct judgment and proper forethought. "Whilst, therefore," says he, " all districts through which our cursory examination has extended *open a fine field for successful enterprise*, and for works of irrigation, there is none, probably, *to which a consolidated company could so well turn their attention as to Scinde*, especially, in the *first instance*, for this reason,—in all such operations as that in which we propose to embark, an unity of action is most desirable, as well as a concentration of our labours and resources." And again—" It is doubtful whether, in any one district *except Scinde*, employment could be found for a large capital on so simple a line of operations, requiring, consequently, only a small staff of executives, and admitting of a development of the system on the largest scale, with the smallest outlay. Were we to undertake several smaller works at once, such as would be sufficient for the employment of a large capital, they would be scattered here and there; would require several, instead of one head executive, and thus, by dividing the points of attention, would multiply the staff and superintendents, and greatly increase the expense." These remarks are well worthy the serious attention of the reader of this pamphlet, and convey an unanswerable argument in favour of the proposed " East India Cotton Company."

Scinde, in consequence of its richness and fertility, has been called *Young Egypt*. The River Indus offers ample means, not merely of inland steam transit but of irrigation on an extensive scale, and to the most beneficial results, if only skilfully attended to. It has also five tributary rivers, capable of fertilising the immense extent of country which they intersect, and of giving the cotton planter *close at hand* all the water he requires with right management. "Water in India," exclaimed Lord Stanley on a recent occasion in the Manchester Town Hall, "is money!" Now, in the Scinde and Punjaub there are, as we have seen, no fewer than six rivers, each of which may—in the language of an eminent Bombay engineer—be made a bank whence boundless wealth may be drawn by the talisman of English capital and skill; in other words, "a well-stored and productive treasury."

A few practical suggestions on irrigation as applicable to the culture of the cotton plant, may possibly not be out of place here, or altogether uninteresting to the reader. Ignorance of the first principles of irrigation has led in many instances which are specially referred to by Dr. Royle in his last publication, to much fruitless expense, and no little disappointment.

The land to be irrigated should be first thoroughly drained to the depth of about 5 feet. It may be here stated that the cotton plant has a tap-root, about $2\frac{1}{2}$ feet in length. When the land becomes properly drained, all the insects which infested it will, when soft, naturally work their way to the surface—the noxious gases will escape—and by the timely application of quick lime, together with the natural power of the sun, the insects can be completely banished. When water is actually required, it must be kept under control by means of flood-gates, so that the water can be increased or diminished in force and quantity, according to the wish of the planter or the requirements of the cotton plant at that particular season. Too much water is as fatal as too little, and engenders an hurtful exuberance of wood and foliage. It must be remembered that this plant only requires four months, under proper treatment, to come to maturity. Careful weeding and attentive hoeing about the plants are necessary. When the pods indicate drooping a want of nourishment is shown, and special care must be observed to gather the pods when they open. Each picker should have three sacks round his neck—one for clean cotton, another for any slightly doubtful in this respect, and the third for the really damaged portion of the crop. I beg to refer the reader, who is anxious to obtain accurate and precise information on the best methods used in the cultivation of the cotton plant and generally employed in America, to a pamphlet on this subject, published at the expense of the " Cotton Supply Association," and written by a late overseer of an American cotton-plantation. The publication in question, I am informed, may be had *gratis* on application to the Secretary of that Association.

Both indigenous and exotic cotton can be grown on the banks of the Indus, and its five tributary rivers, at a less cost and in larger quantities than in any other part of the world. And I feel certain, both from personal observation whilst employed in Her Majesty's service in India and from extensive reading on the subject, that in these provinces at least as much cotton can be grown, acre for acre, as in the Southern States of America. The following facts, to a great extent, bear me out in the opinion I have long entertained of the immense *cotton-productiveness* of British India, aided by irrigation and proper methods of culture.

From a careful report on the cotton plants grown on the Government farms in the South Mahratta country, in 1844, it was ascertained that of seed-cotton, Broach yielded, *per acre*, 251℔; Coimbatore, 360℔; Native Dharwar, 220℔; and Dharwar American or New Orleans, 350℔ to 400℔.

Mr. D. Lees, of Manchester, who went to India in 1849 for the benefit of his health, and settled in the Tinnivelly district, commenced growing cotton from *New Orleans seed*, at Pamuagoody, and also on the sea-coast, near Trichendore; and he reported that in a very short time he succeeded in collecting at the rate of 500℔ or 600℔ per acre.

From experiments made at Coimbatore, by Mr. Wroughton and Dr. Wight, from 681℔ to 1,100℔ of seed-cotton per acre were obtained; and they discovered that they could ship to Liverpool this very excellent exotic or American cotton, all expenses included, for 3½d. per lb, and realise a good profit. This was in 1850.

Mr. Elphinstone, in one of the districts of the Bombay Presidency below the Ghauts, obtained 166lb per beegah even of *Sea Island cotton*, which was pronounced by the Bombay Chamber of Commerce alike beautiful in staple, colour, and fineness, as well as free from impurity of any kind.

Fortunately for the cotton spinners of Lancashire, New Orleans cotton gives, *on Indian soil*, a larger yield per acre, and more wool in proportion to the seed, than cotton of native growth;—fortunately, I say, because this particular description is well known to be in the best request, and consumed in the largest quantities, by the English manufacturer. "By reference to the Parliamentary Report of 1848 (Quest. 3783-3786), we find that while it required thirteen acres of land to produce a candy of 784lb of clean indigenous cotton, the same quantity of New Orleans was grown upon seven acres; and taking the price at which Government contracted with the ryots for cultivating the land at 3s. per acre, and adding to it the assessment of 3s., the cost of cultivating an acre of land is 6s. Consequently, if we can grow the same quantity of New Orleans on seven acres as can be produced on thirteen acres from the native seed, we thereby effect a clear saving of 36s.; or, in other words, we nearly double the crop."

* See "Cotton Crisis," page 16.

Besides which, this class of cotton is more easily cultivated, requiring little irrigation or artificial aid, and its marketable value is higher by 40 or 50 per cent, than that of the native growths.

In a letter which appeared in the *Manchester Guardian*, dated 21st February, 1848 (more than ten years ago), Mr. John Peel stated that "the quality of cotton grown from the New Orleans seed, in India, is now well known in Bombay, and that, while the highest quotations of Surats were 74 rupees, cotton from New Orleans seed was quoted at 114 rupees. The return to the cultivator, upon an acre of ground, is thus doubled, for he gets 50 per cent more weight of cotton, and an increase of 50 per cent in value."

Mr. Mercer reported the same facts to the East India Company. He said that "plants from the New Orleans seed, grown at Coimbatore, produced seed which, when planted at Dharwar, produced even finer cotton than the fresh seed;" and that "the natives who cultivated it made nearly 50 per cent more than they did on cotton produced from native seed."

Perhaps the reader may here be disposed to ask,— "You have plainly shown that India can be made to produce as much cotton, acre for acre, as the United States, and that too of the same kind or class of cotton most in demand in the English market (viz., New Orleans), but can you ship it from Kurrachee to Liverpool, and afford to sell it at a lower price than can the American planters or brokers?" Alexander

Nesbit Shaw, Esq., late Revenue Commissioner in the Northern District of India, states it as his opinion that it can be grown in India and sold in Manchester for *less than 2d. per ℔, with a profit to all parties.* Dr. Wight states that it can be landed at Liverpool for 3½d. per ℔; and Dr. Royle informs us that " some of this cotton was sold at Bombay for 113 rupees a candy;" and that " 500 bales of it were sent to Manchester for 6½d. per ℔, which cost about 3½d.," thus making the nett gain of the Bombay purchaser nearly 3d. per ℔, or 100 per cent.

Mr. Mackay, the late Commissioner to India of the Manchester, Liverpool, Blackburn, and Glasgow Chambers of Commerce, has stated that upon a mere yield of 70℔ per acre, or a total of 560℔, at 3d. per ℔, the profit arising from the cultivation of *eight acres of land*, even allowing three rupees for interest of borrowed money, is not less than 41 rupees. According to this calculation (which is certainly far below the mark, either as respects the quantity grown per acre, or the real money-value of the cotton itself), a public company cultivating a few thousand acres would realise a colossal annual dividend; and if to the operations of this supposed company should be added the purchase of cotton in exchange or barter for Manchester grey and bleached goods, a double profit, amounting to not less than 50 per cent annually upon the capital invested, would at the very least be realised under good and economical management.

In fact, as has been truly remarked, " such are the

boundless capabilities of soil and climate that India possesses, that, were they skilfully developed and vigorously wrought,—were the proper growths of cotton introduced, in place of the indigenous plant, and the process placed under efficient management, and due encouragement given to the native cultivator,—not only could India furnish all we require for the purposes of home manufacture, but she could ultimately *supply cotton of the best quality at lower prices* than are now charged by *the planters* of the United States, and, consequently, *could undersell and supersede them in the market."*

The reader, will, I trust, have been convinced by the preceding statements, confirmed by the most eminent authorities on every particular discussed, that the only means wanting to convert India into the cotton-field of England and, perhaps, of the world, is the immediate and consolidated application of English capital, enterprise, and skill. Hence it is that I propose the formation of an association, to be entitled " The East India Cotton Company," under the " Limited Liability Act," with a capital of £1,000,000, in shares of £10 each, for the purpose of growing cotton in the provinces of Scinde and the Punjaub, with a central depôt at Kurrachee, consisting of gins, hydraulic presses, &c., &c., and, also, of purchasing cotton of the native cultivators, either for money or in exchange for British manufactures. I am informed by a Manchester mercantile firm, who have a large establishment at Kurrachee, that they find that the native dealers in cotton show a decided preference for barter, and had much rather have, instead of money, Lancashire grey and bleached goods at the prices affixed to them (which, nevertheless, leave a profit to the firm in question of from 30 to 40 per cent., after paying all expenses,) in exchange for their raw cotton. The whole cost of this cotton at Liverpool (freightage and brokerage included) does not exceed 3d. or $3\frac{1}{4}$d. per ℔, so that there is here an ample margin for profit, in addition to the 30 or 40 per cent made on the goods forwarded from Manchester to Kurrachee.

I have already entered into negotiations with this firm for the purchase of their three hydraulic presses, and the whole of their establishment at Kurrachee (which immediately adjoins the railway station there), in order that the above Company may commence immediate operations upon the first instalment being subscribed—viz., 30s. per share. This instalment, and 5s. per share application or deposit fee, will be all that will be required for the first year, as the same will amount to £175,000. Should the quantity, however, of cotton offered for sale to the agents of the Company exceed the quantity taken into calculation by the directors as the probable purchase for the first year, not more than a second instalment would be required to meet the extra supply of this article. And even in this case the shareholders would be gainers, inasmuch as their profits would swell in proportion, and make a better dividend.

I may likewise add that as the Company are assured of extensive grants of land, *in perpetuity*, being made to them by the Indian Government, no portion of their capital will be required in the *purchase of soil for cultivation*.

I have made applications to the East India Company and the Board of Control—Firstly, that a grant of land, *in perpetuity*, should be made to this Company for the cultivation of cotton, on a large experimental and remunerative basis ; and secondly, that the Company should be able to purchase land of the natives, with a fee-simple title. From both these high official sources, I have had the honour to receive favourable replies, only it appears that, as a matter of form or etiquette, application must be made to the local government in India to give, ratify, or confirm a charter in pursuance of the objects above stated. The selection of the land will, however, have to be made by the " East India Cotton Company," in order to free the Indian Government from any responsibility in the matter. There will be no difficulty in selecting a vast tract of suitable and congenial soil, in the peaceful valley of the Indus, or, in other words, in Scinde and the Punjaub, for the purpose of cultivating cotton for the English market, as these provinces contain more land adapted for this purpose than, perhaps, the whole of the Southern States of America, with a superabundance of adult labour at 3d. or 4d. per diem, and every desirable means both of irrigation and transit at command. In the Appendix will be found copies of my letters to Lord Ellenborough (then President of the Board of Control), and the Court of Directors of the East India Company, and also of their several replies, furnishing every legitimate ground for inferring that the Bombay Government is formally instructed to accede to my wishes, and to give every possible encouragement to the Company, in its proposed investment of capital and skill in the cultivation of the American cotton plant on the banks of the Indus, admitted by all competent judges to afford the best sites that could possibly be selected in all India for agricultural operations *on a large scale*, both as regard their natural productiveness, when aided by a little irrigation, and their general geographical advantages.

The following facts will, it is hoped, satisfy the English capitalist that the concluding statement in my last paragraph is based on the best evidence, and can admit scarcely of a doubt.

Kurrachee—a fine sea harbour, and likely to become the most frequented in all Asia—is within 600 miles of the Persian Gulf, and connected already by railway with the Indus at Hydrabad. As a commercial entrepôt for the countries east and west of the Indus, it presents advantages and facilities superior to Bombay itself.

The Scinde and Punjaub Railway flotilla are shortly intended to ply on the Indus, and to communicate with Kurrachee and the Persian Gulf. This noble river will, there is ample evidence to prove, become eventually the main artery of the commerce of Asia.

Scinde is not alone the best district in India for the growth of cotton, but it is one where the facilities for embarking the produce are the greatest. Kurrachee is fast becoming the port of shipment for the merchandise, not merely of Scinde, but of the Punjaub and the whole of Central Asia. The Indus is now navigated by steamers of large tonnage, and up to Kurrachee the river is of sufficient depth to allow vessels of great draught to be navigated.* When the projected line of railway up the valley of the Euphrates shall be completed, the transit of goods will be rendered comparatively expeditious between the Indus and England; but I believe that ere long a better means of communication between those places than even that railway will be adopted, namely, water carriage the whole distance. It is well known that the main obstacle to this mode of conveyance is the shallowness of the bed of the river Euphrates. Now the waters of this river and the Tigris run parallel to each other at a short distance, and those of the former could, at no great cost or labour, be turned into the bed of the latter river. When Queen Nictoeris, Regent during the minority of her son, Belshazzar, resolved to construct large quays at Babylon, on the banks of the River Euphrates, she turned that river, by a canal, into the Tigris, and thoroughly dried it. This canal was partly closed up when Cyrus invested Babylon, but he re-opened it, and marched his army to the attack of Babylon

* 26 feet at high tide.

through the dry bed of the Euphrates. Thus the channel of the Euphrates could be deepened up to Belis, the present port on the river for small steamers, so as to admit the passage of vessels of large burden from Kurrachee down the Indus, across the Arabian Sea, up the Persian Gulf and thence along the Euphrates to Belis. From this place to the Mediterranean Sea the distance is less than 100 miles by way of Aleppo. Most of the distance is along valleys where a ship or other canal could be formed without meeting any extraordinary engineering difficulties. But even if this plan should be found impracticable, the goods coming by the steamers up the river might be conveyed across land to the Mediterranean by the railway projected between Selencia, on the coast of Syria, and the Euphrates. To increase the depth of the bed of this river would, in my opinion, cost much less than the making of a railway along the valley of the Euphrates, which when made would require yearly a great outlay in keeping in repair, and other contingent expenses. The advantages of this route are infinitely superior to that by way of Suez and is shorter by 1,400 miles. which is a most important consideration.

Kurrachee is likewise intended to be the station for telegraphic communication between England and the whole of India. Already the telegraph is at work between these islands and Constantinople; and the materials for forming the line thence to the head of the Persian Gulf have, by direction of the Turkish

Government, been lately forwarded from this country and will immediately be laid down, so that there only remains a distance of 1,200 miles from the terminus of the Turkish telegraph line to Kurrachee, in which the cable can easily be laid and at a comparatively small expense. But to lay the telegraphic cable by way of Suez would require a length of 5.000 miles, much of it in the Red Sea where the difficulties are almost, if not altogether, insurmountable, as is most ably shown by Mr. Andrew, the Chairman of the Euphrates Valley Railway Company.

But even independent of these advantages, Kurrachee is at this moment the European port of India. Instead of the produce of Scinde and the Punjaub being shipped as formerly to Bombay for re-shipment to England, it is now transmitted direct, and Kurrachee is destined to become the Liverpool of India.

Since the conquest of that country, the trade of Scinde, despite all obstacles, has advanced at the rate of 575 per cent, and is capable of an indefinite extension and of a very rapid development by the application of English capital and energy. The value of the exports of wool alone has increased in the last five years from 7, 57, 162 rupees, to 31, 15, 903 rupees, an increase equivalent to 312 per cent.

P. M. Dalzell, Esq., Deputy-Collector of Customs at Kurrachee, informs us that "The value of the trade of Scinde now amounts to a million and a half sterling, exclusive of the value of government stores. If it progress within the next four years in the ratio

D

of the past two, in 1860, even under present circumstances, it will exceed three millions and a half sterling, or three-tenths the present value of the trade
of Bombay, deducting the value (Rs. 3, 13, 27, 682)
of her imports re-exported,—Scinde having no such
feature in her trade of any consequence to give
it a fictitious value,—and when the lines of railway
in the Punjaub and Scinde shall be open to traffic;
the river communication improved by convenient and
powerful steamers; and the harbour made eligible
for vessels of deeper draft—Kurrachee cannot fail to
become one of the chief commercial cities of the
empire."

It is here that the " East India Cotton Company" pro-
poses to establish its depôt; and the close connection
of this city, by water and railway, with the great cotton-
growing districts of Scinde and the Punjaub, of Cutch,
Candeish, and other adjoining provinces (not excepting
Affghanistan), ensures every facility and convenience
for successful enterprise, both as regard the purchase
of cotton from the native cultivators on an extensive
scale for export direct to England, and the sale or
barter of British manufactures to the traders from all
the surrounding countries, from Upper India and from
Persia itself. For the reader must remember that
a saving of 17 per cent will be effected by simply
shipping produce at Kurrachee direct to England,
instead of sending it to Bombay for shipment thence;
and that (as Mr. Dalzell confidently states) so soon as
the traders find that they can procure as cheap and

equally good articles at Kurrachee as at Bombay, so surely will they abandon the latter market for the former.

These considerations strongly incline me to the opinion that it would be highly judicious and profitable for the " East India Cotton Company" to open a large bazaar at Kurrachee for the reception, *on agency charges*, of all kinds of British goods suitable to the India market. This is a matter, however, for the serious consideration of the future Board of Directors, who will adopt only such measures as the greatest prudence and foresight, together with the amplest information, will perfectly justify, and the soundest experience warrant. Still it is an universally-acknowledged fact, that the natives of India are inordinately fond of British manufactures ; and that the want of means, and not of inclination, alone prevents them from becoming the best customers under the sun for the products of English labour and skill. Among a population composed of *two hundred millions*, there is no doubt but that an enormous and highly profitable system of traffic would be established, in an incredibly short period, by the proposed Company stationing each of their agents in the centre of a large cotton district, with a store of goods always at hand, and prepared to make advances both of goods and money to the ryots, in the proportion of two-thirds of the value of their cotton crops, then supposed to be maturing. The carrying out of a system of this kind on the safest principles of

barter, together with the establishment of a central
bazaar for the use of the residents and traders from
remote provinces, could not fail to be attended with
enormous profits, and to give such an impetus to the
trade and agriculture of the valley of the Indus and
regions beyond, as has had no parallel in the history
of this superb dependency.

The soil of this part of India is capable of returning
three harvests in the year, and is altogether out of
the reach of the monsoon, so fatal and destructive
in other parts of the East. The *adjoining* provinces
of Cutch, Guzerat, and Candeish called from its
fertility the *Garden of the East*, contain thousands of
miles of excellent cotton land, and already produce large quantities, principally for consumption
by the native manfacturers. Cutch, the adjoining
province to Scinde, exported last year to Bombay
cotton wool that amounted to upwards of one-sixth
the produce of the Bombay Presidency : and all the
cotton grown in these districts is expected very shortly
to be imported into Kurrachee as being the nearest
market. As soon as the Company commence operations, and set to work a proper number of hydraulic
presses, all this valuable produce will come into their
hands to be packed for export to England, and a
large and profitable business can immediately be
embarked in.

A correspondent of an Indian paper wrote in 1855,
as follows :—" Along the banks of our Punjaub rivers
lie tracts of land *admirably adapted for the growth of*

cotton. It only requires steady encouragement on the part of the local government, trouble and perseverance on the part of the district officer, *to cover those lands with cotton of the finest quality."* He further states that "the cotton that could thus be grown might, with ease and at trifling a cost, be conveyed down the Indus to Kurrachee, and there shipped for England;" and adds, " Kurrachee is a port of great importance, but, like many things of great importance, not heeded or taken advantage of. The one article, cotton, if properly cultivated in the Punjaub and in Scinde, would afford export freight for a vast number of ships visiting Kurrachee, while government stores for the Punjaub, private property and merchandise, would afford endless import freight, to say nothing of the great number of passengers who would avail themselves of that route."

Cotton is brought to Scinde right across the Jaysulmere Desert from Rajpootana; and we are informed by a Scinde newspaper, that " any one located on the banks of the River Indus might observe fleets of boats coming down the river in the winter months, *all laden with cotton."*

That exotic cotton, of an excellent marketable quality in the English market, can be easily grown in the two great provinces which I have selected for the scene of the Company's agricultural operations, is evident from the following statement by a correspondent of an Indian paper :—" In April last (1855) I brought to England a small quantity of cotton (the raw material) grown from *acclimated* American cotton seed, in a district on the banks of the River Jhelum; this specimen I had shown to several cotton spinners in Manchester. They pronounced it to be the finest specimen of cotton they had seen grown in India, even directly from American seed, and to be worth from 6¼d. to 6½d. per ℔." The same cotton would now be worth 8d. per ℔ in the Liverpool market, or more.

The benefits which it is fairly to be presumed will follow upon the operations of the " East India Cotton Company," may be stated briefly as follows :—

1. A cessation to our present criminal participation in the guilt of perpetuating slavery in the Southern States of America.

2. The transfer of the immense capital, annually expended by our cotton spinners in the purchase of cotton, *from* America (a rival nation), *to* our own Empire in the East.

3. A great and desirable amelioration in the condition of the poor ryots of India, by putting an end to the cruel oppression and base extortions of their tyrants—the money-lenders—and thus giving them a more direct interest in the cultivation of the soil, and more especially of the cotton plant. This of itself would do more to tranquilise the Indian people, and bend them to our rule, than a host of armies or the entire paraphernalia of internal government.

4. The protection of British commerce and manufactures from the evil effects of a diminution in the supply of raw cotton.

5. The healthy expansion of the factory system throughout the whole of our textile districts, and the consequent increased employment of the working population. Yes, the operatives of this kingdom are personally and deeply interested in the successful formation and proposed operations of this Company; and to them I appeal for collective and intelligent support. Their destinies are involved in the development of the great cotton-growing capabilities of British India; and, indeed, there is no other section of the community whose interests will be better protected, or more largely promoted, by the present undertaking, because there are none so fearfully jeopardised by any uncertainty in the supply of the raw material from America, which we have proved to be necessary to their very existence, comfort, and social progress. Upon the slightest failure in the cotton crops on the banks of the Mississippi, the usual demand ceases for their labour; the short-time system is introduced; and poverty, involuntary idleness, and decreasing wages, are the inevitable consequences.

6. The greatly-increased consumption of our manufactured goods, on the part of *two hundred millions* of the inhabitants of our Eastern Empire, and the inevitable extension of our shipping and mercantile, as well as industrial, prosperity.

In fact, to diffuse universal prosperity throughout the United Kingdom, and to develope the rich resources of a hitherto neglected dependency,—in other words, to extend agriculture and trade, to succour the oppressed and provide employment for the industrious in both hemispheres,—are *desiderata* well worthy the sanction and support of all classes of the British community. And such are the objects the promoters of the " East India Cotton Company" have in view.

Unlike many other projects, this is free from all conjecture or doubt. We know the geographical advantages of Scinde and the Punjaub. We know the fertility of the valley of the Indus, and all along the banks of the five tributary rivers ; and that the means of irrigation and water transit are most ample. We know that these provinces are out of the reach of the heavy monsoons so destructive to the cotton crops of other parts of India, and from frosts so fatal in America. We know that not only is the cotton plant indigenous, but that here can be grown, at little cost, the best varieties from Mexican seed.* We know that there is more land intersected by the Indus than there is now under cotton cultivation in the United States. We know that the immense tracts of cotton land in the surrounding provinces, nay, throughout India, will ere long be connected with the Indus (north and south) in one continuous line of railway.† We know that on this noble river is about to be plied the light-draught steamers of the " Oriental Inland Steam Company," and the steam flotilla† of " The Scinde and Punjaub Railway ;" and that, by the means of

* See Appendix for Mr. Paske's Report.—Extract from Dr. Royle's Pamphlet.

† See Appendix.

these steam boats, a direct intercourse will be opened
between Kurrachee and the Persian Gulf, bringing
the former as near to England as America is by the
present route. These are facts " patent to the world,"
and most of them amply proved by Lieut.-Col. Grant,
in his excellent pamphlet on "Irrigation." Sure am
I that the "East India Cotton Company," by availing
itself of all these advantages, and not merely growing
but purchasing cotton on a gigantic scale, and,
through its agents, bartering British manufactures*
for the produce of the Indian planter, will, before
twelve months expire, realise an enormous profit, and
pay a larger dividend to its shareholders than any
other public undertaking of the kind has hitherto
done. It is not a mere local or ordinary speculation,
but one of *national* importance; and capable of
affecting *for good* the political, as well as the commercial, destinies of Great Britain, as well as of her
gigantic possessions in the East; and, in fact, of
working out a new and better epoch in the future
industrial annals of both hemispheres.

How, I ask, has America become the great *cotton-
producer* of the world? I answer, by the dint of her
enterprise, industry, and perseverance. The cotton
at first exported from her shores to this country was
of a very inferior description to that now landed in
the Liverpool market from Bombay; improved
methods of cultivation, as in every branch of agriculture, soon led to a supply of superior varieties,

* See Appendix.

adapted to the production of all kinds of English cotton fabric, from the plainest calico to the finest muslin. Let the cotton spinners of Lancashire take a lesson from the history of their young and Transatlantic rival, and apply it, as best they can, to the development of the great cotton-growing capabilities of British India.

Having thus briefly, but, I trust, satisfactorily shown that Scinde and the Punjaub are admirably adapted for the growth of cotton on a large and remunerative basis—that Kurrachee possesses ample and unparalleled advantages as the entrepôt and head-quarters of the Company's operations—and that all the desired facilities for irrigation and water and railway conveyance are at immediate command and to any extent—I may further remark that the valley of the Indus has been spared, by the docility and loyalty of its inhabitants, any part whatever in the mutinous disaffection to the English Government which has desolated Bengal, and is now rampant in Oude and throughout various other provinces of this colossal empire. This is a consideration of paramount importance, and, coupled with the known patient and industrious habits of the population of Scinde and the Punjaub, and the extremely cheap rate at which adult labour can be had in super-abundance, irrefragably demonstrates that in all essential points these provinces present the most tempting and congenial field to English enterprise and skill. Not merely by these means would boundless wealth be achieved:

but the same means would, rapidly and systematically, develope the rich resources and vast cotton-growing capabilities of this truly *peaceful valley of the Indus*, peopled, east and west, by a race proverbial for docility, patience, and industry.

The reader of this pamphlet will not be surprised, therefore, to learn that my project has been approved of highly by the East India Company, the Manchester Cotton Supply Association, and the leading Chambers of Commerce in the emporiums of British industry and merchandise; and that I am in the daily habit of receiving letters from statesmen, capitalists, and the most intelligent merchants and manufacturers we have amongst us in its favour, each of them containing pledges of unqualified support. It would require a volume to lay before the public the mass of correspondence in my possession, and in the hands of Mr. Collinson, the Secretary to this Company; but, in order to satisfy the reader on this head, I shall give in the Appendix brief extracts from the communications of the following gentlemen, which are strongly indicative of the general impression that the present undertaking will be attended with the *best possible results*, not merely to the individual shareholder, but to India and Great Britain at large; viz:—Alexander Nesbit Shaw, Esq., late Commissioner of Revenue in the Northern District of India; W. P. Andrew, Esq., the Chairman of the Scinde and Punjaub Railway, the Euphrates Valley Railway Company, &c., &c.;

Sir James Brooke, K.C.B., Rajah of Sarawak; Mr.
Ennis, M.P. (for Athlone), and Governor of the
Bank of Ireland; the Right Hon. T. M. Gibson,
M.P.; Lieut.-Col. Grimes, Hon. E.I.C.S., Deputy-
Chairman of the Oriental Inland Steam Company;
H. Dunlop, Esq., of Glasgow; Edmund Ashworth,
Esq ,Vice-President of the Cotton Supply Association;
H. Rumboldt, Esq., Grove House, Cleckheaton; W. E.
Forster, Esq., Burley, Yorkshire, and the author
of a most excellent lecture on India; and Thomas
Emmott, Esq., Albion and Vale Mills, Oldham. It
is presumed that the extracts given in the Appendix
from the communications of these gentlemen, will
be amply sufficient to show that the "East India
Cotton Company" is no chimerical project, but is
entitled to public support, especially in the cotton-
manufacturing districts, and among all classes of
English capitalists who are desirous to emancipate
Great Britain from her present abject and dangerous
dependence on America for the chief, nay, almost
sole, supply of the raw material necessary to the
maintenance of her national industry and commerce,
and the well-being of the entire community, from the
highest to the lowest.

Having thus, I trust, clearly and satisfactorily shown
the folly of exposing the cotton trade of this kingdom
to endless fluctuation, and liability to ruin and decay,
from a deficient crop in the Southern States of
America, and the fact of their having reached the maximum, the highest attainable limit, of their productive

power; the necessity of sacrificing our national honour for the maintenance of amicable relations with a foreign Government, which, by withholding cotton from our dominions, could lay prostrate in the dust the whole fabric of our manufacturing and commercial supremacy; the direct identification of the cotton spinners of Great Britain with the infamous system of Transatlantic slavery deprecated by the wise and good of all Christian nations; the easiest and most effectual means of freeing the slave from his accursed thraldom, and restoring to him the rights and privileges of humanity, of which the cotton planter has deprived him, in order to minister to the wants of *Christian* England; the progressive and fatal rivalry of American manufactures in markets once our exclusive possession; the threatening decrease in the export of cotton from New York and New Orleans to our shores; the sound policy of encouraging colonisation in our vast Eastern Empire, and its boundless capabilities of soil and climate for the production of cotton of all desirable qualities, and to an extent commensurate with the wants of the English manufacturers; the difficulties to be overcome, and the means to be employed, for the development of the resources of India, and the indefinite expansion of the cotton industry at home; and, above all, the claims of the "East India Cotton Company" to the undivided support of British capitalists, the friends of negro emancipation, all sincere patriots, and especially the cotton spinners of Manchester and Glasgow; as well as the certainty of this undertaking being attended with immense profit to its members, and of unparalleled service, not merely to Scinde and the Punjaub, but to British manufactures and commerce in all their ramifications and results. I say, I trust, having clearly and satisfactorily established these points, that the readers of this pamphlet will heartily and combinedly enter on a career of successful enterprise that shall elevate India above America as a cotton-producing country, and render Great Britain independent of *any foreign source* for the supply of the fibre that maintains in motion the whole machinery of her industrial and mercantile greatness.

It is in our power to make our Eastern Empire supply the wants of Lancashire and of the world, and, if we do not do so, great is our folly and enormous our guilt! For, says Mr. Shaw (the best authority on this subject), "It is my full and firm belief that India can produce cotton equal to the American Upland, Mobile, or New Orleans, and at *less than half the cost.* And I indulge the hope, improbable as it may now appear, that Indian cotton may ultimately oust the American from the English markets; and it is by no means impossible that we may yet supply America herself. Then let us not delay putting our shoulders energetically to the wheel. The game is in our hands, *if we are only determined to play it out."*

THE EAST INDIA COTTON COMPANY.

(LIMITED.)

CAPITAL, £1,000,000 ; IN 100,000 SHARES OF £10 EACH.

This Company is formed for the cultivation and purchase of cotton in India.

The importance of an increased supply of cotton is notorious, and admits of no doubt. That the power of consumption threatens to exceed the production of the raw material has become a matter of national alarm; and it is now universally conceded that so serious a catastrophe can only be averted by European capital, skill, and energy being directed to the cultivation of the cotton plant in countries specially adapted—by soil and climate—to its profitable and abundant growth.

We have it on indisputable authority that if the increase in the power of consumption in England alone continues for the next twenty years, at the same comparative rate it has progressed since 1850, *five million bales* of cotton will be required from America to keep up her present relative proportion of supply. But can America produce this progressively-estimated quantity? She has never yet grown 3,250,000 bales, of which she has retained for her own consumption an annually-augmented proportion; and still, of 900,000,000 lb, imported in 1856 into this country, she supplied us with 700,000,000 lb. This is a state of things that cannot last, and should not if it could, because it exposes the cotton manufacture of Great Britain to constant and imminent peril—to ceaseless fluctuations in the price and quantity of the raw material—and, in case of a deficient crop, a revolt among the slave population, or a diplomatic quarrel, to the utter prostration of the national resources.

It has been stated, by the Vice-President of the "Cotton Supply Association" (Edmund Ashworth, Esq.), that a rise of 1d. in the pound, on raw cotton imported into the United Kingdom, amounts to a difference in its money-value of £5,000,000. According to this mode of computation, the increase in the price of this raw material, between 1845 and 1857, is equivalent to a tax upon the industry of Great Britain of *twenty millions sterling per annum.* At the former period, New Orleans was worth 4d. per lb—at the latter period, it was just double—and even, at the enormous price of 8d. per lb, the supply is necessarily limited and uncertain. The uncertainty of the supply is the chief element in the excessive dearness which is so fatal to our manufacturing prosperity.

Mr. Bazley informed the "Manchester Chamber of Commerce," at its last annual meeting, that, after a very careful analysis, he found that in cotton, in silk, in flax, in dyes, in oils, and other materials that enter into our manufactures, a sum was paid of £50,000,000 per annum, or *one million sterling per week*, in excess of what ought to be paid ; and this he attributed to our English capitalists (especially those most interested in the trade) not having invested any portion of their surplus-wealth in the production and increase of these raw materials. The "East India Cotton Company" offers a remedy to the evil so far as cotton is concerned ; and by the scientific and improved cultivation of "India's native plant," will inaugurate a new era in our domestic manufactures, and hasten the event foretold by the late Mr. Mackay (then Commissioner to India of the Manchester, Liverpool, Blackburn, and Glasgow Chambers of Commerce), viz., that the day is not far distant when Lowell itself will be indebted to India for *cheap cotton.*

The cost of cultivating cotton in America is 60s. per acre, or 3d. per ℔ to the planter. In India the cost is under 9s. per acre, and the ryot can afford his cotton at from 1d. to 1½d. per ℔ at the place of production. Even now, in the far interior, notwithstanding the enormous charge of conveyance on bullocks' backs to the seaport, and of freightage and insurance to England, it can be produced at a profit, if sold at 3½d. per ℔ in Liverpool.

Mr. Mercer, one of the American cultivators employed by the East India Company, states in his report, October, 1844, that "India cotton has long been known to possess two very remarkable qualities: it mills or swells in bleaching, thereby yielding a more substantial fabric; it takes and retains colour better than American cotton, and hence would command a good market, provided it were sent in regular supply and of uniform cleanness."

New Orleans cotton is worth 2d. per ℔ more than Surats in the Liverpool market; but then the inferiority of the latter is more owing to its dirty or adulterated condition than to its inherent value as a fibre were it only properly cultivated, cleaned, and prepared for shipment. Indian soil can be made to grow cotton, from American seed, of as good marketable quality as Louisiana or Georgia. All that is required is a better mode of cultivating, gathering, and storing, under European supervision; of separating the fibre from the seed, and of packing the produce clean for transmission abroad; and when these points are accomplished—and not till then—America will find in India a powerful competitor in European markets, and England the best customer for her manufactures.

The part of India selected for the field of cultivation by the "East India Cotton Company" is in the Scinde and Punjaub territories, on the banks of the Indus and her five tributary streams, which is unrivalled in position, fertility of soil, and climate, being situated out of the reach of the monsoon, so fatal and destructive in other portions of the East, and commanding abundant irrigation, and cheap and inexhaustible labour, capable of producing more cotton than the whole of the American Slave States, and at less price than it can be grown for in any other quarter of the globe.

A railway is already completed connecting Hyderabad with the fine harbour of Kurrachee, near to the Persian Gulf, besides another line of railway, in process of construction, uniting the whole of the cotton districts, and terminating at Lahore, on the Indus.

During the present fearful insurrection, the native inhabitants of Scinde and the Punjaub have not only remained faithful to us, but have been our steady allies.

These are advantages all combined that render the site selected the finest in India for the growth of cotton on an extensive and remunerative scale. It will be a still more favourable locality for the purposes of the "East India Cotton Company" when the "Oriental Inland Steam Navigation Company" ply their steamers on the noble Indus. It is not improbable that both companies may commence direct operations about the same period.

Promise of support has been received from the "Cotton Supply Association," and letters of approval from several Chambers of Commerce.

The East India Company have been applied to for free grants of land, which have been liberally accorded, subject to the selection of the same by Captain Collins, the projector and representative of the Company.

Each applicant for shares will be required to accompany his application with five shillings per share, on the number of shares applied for, for which a voucher in each case will be given, or sent per post. On allotment, the further sum of 30s. per share will have to be paid to one of the Bankers of the Company, and no second call will be made in less than three months' time therefrom.

In the event of the Directors allotting to the applicant less than the whole number of shares applied for, the amount of 5s. per share will be appropriated towards the instalment due immediately on allotment.

As soon as a sufficient number of shares is applied for, the allotment will immediately take place. A Board of Management will very shortly be announced; and the Company duly registered. Apply to Mr. Edward Collinson, Secretary to the Promoters, Town Hall Buildings, 57, Cross Street, Manchester.